Otter B
JOYFUL

WRITTEN BY
Pamela Kennedy & Anne Kennedy Brady

ILLUSTRATED BY
Aaron Zenz

Tyndale

Tyndale House Publishers, Inc.
Carol Stream, Illinois

FOCUS ON THE FAMILY®

Otter B: Joyful
© Pamela Kennedy and Anne Kennedy Brady. All rights reserved.
Illustrations © 2021 Focus on the Family

A Focus on the Family book published by Tyndale House Publishers,
Carol Stream, Illinois 60188

Focus on the Family and the accompanying logo and design are federally
registered trademarks of Focus on the Family, 8605 Explorer Drive,
Colorado Springs, CO 80920.

TYNDALE and Tyndale's quill logo are registered trademarks of
Tyndale House Ministries.

Cover design by Josh Lewis
Cover illustration by Aaron Zenz

Book design by Josh Lewis
Text set in Source Sans and Prater Sans Pro.

For manufacturing information regarding this product, please call
1-855-277-9400.

For information about special discounts for bulk purchases, please contact
Tyndale House Publishers at csresponse@tyndale.com, or call 1-855-277-9400.

Library of Congress Cataloging-in-Publication Data can be found at
www.loc.gov.

ISBN 978-1-64607-038-1

Printed in China

27 26 25 24 23 22 21
7   6   5   4   3   2   1

"Places, everyone!"
called Mr. Mallard, the Sunday
school teacher.

"This is our last rehearsal
before the Christmas
play tomorrow night!"

"Can you tighten my halo?" Tabitha asked.
Otter B retied the silvery string that held a
circle of tinsel on Tabitha's head.

"Thanks!" She skipped off to the other side of the stage. Then she practiced waving around her stick with all the glittery stars.

Otter B hugged his stuffed sheep and watched everyone get ready.

Felicia draped a pretty blue shawl across her shoulders and swished her tail.

"Franklin!" she called. "Mary and Joseph are married, so you have to stay next to me!"

Franklin hopped over. He wore his dad's bathrobe and pulled his brother's toy horse behind him.

"Cool sheep, Otter B," Roscoe said, adjusting his gold crown.
"Thanks," Otter B shrugged. "What's in that box?"

"Gold and nonsense for Baby Jesus,"
he replied.

"Frankincense, Roscoe!"
said Felicia.

Mr. Mallard clapped twice. "Okay, everyone, let's get started!"

Franklin hopped forward and cleared his throat. "Come, Mary. We need to go to Bethlehem because that's where my family is from. You can ride this donkey."

Franklin rolled the horse to Felicia and they walked across the stage.

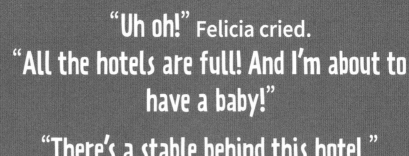

"Uh oh!" Felicia cried.
"All the hotels are full! And I'm about to
have a baby!"

"There's a stable behind this hotel,"
said Franklin.

"Great!" Felicia said.
They sat in a pile of
straw next to a large
wooden cow.

Then Felicia held up a doll she'd brought from home.
"Hooray! My baby is born!"
She put the doll into the cow's feeding trough.

Franklin gazed at the doll.
"An angel said we should call Him Jesus, so let's do that."
Felicia nodded.

Otter B sat at the side of the stage beside his stuffed sheep. Tabitha climbed up on a bench in front of him.

"Behold!" she shouted. "We bring you good tidings of great joy! God's Son, Jesus, was born in Bethlehem tonight. Look for a baby in a manger. And hurry up!"

Tabitha the angel dashed over to the stable and held her stars above Franklin and Felicia. Otter B carried his sheep over to them.
"Can I see your baby?" he asked.
"I heard His name is Jesus."

Felicia held up the baby doll. "He sure is cute," Otter B said.
"Baaaaaa," said his sheep.

Then Roscoe walked importantly across the stage.

"I have followed yonder star across the desert," he announced. "I have brought gold and nonsense for your baby."

"Thank you, oh wise man, for the gold and frankincense," Felicia said, rolling her eyes.

Then everyone sang "Away in a Manger."

As they put away their costumes and props, Tabitha
handed Otter B her wings. Otter B sighed.
"I wish I could be an angel. Or a Wise Guy."

"Why? The shepherds were the coolest!"
Tabitha said.

"No, they weren't," said Otter B. "All they did was go look at Baby Jesus."

"Yeah, but then right afterward, they went all over the place telling people what happened! They were the first ones to tell everyone that Jesus was born!"

Otter B skipped all the way home beside Mama.

As soon as they walked through the door, Otter B grabbed some Christmas paper, star stickers, and markers, and went to work.

"Mama," he called after a while. "I'm going to deliver some Christmas joy, just like the shepherds did!"

Otter B hopped on his bike and took off. He delivered one of his handmade Christmas cards to every neighbor.

When he came back home, Mama gave him a mug of cocoa with whipped cream on top.

"That was so much fun," he said, giggling when the whipped cream stuck to his nose.

"I get to be a shepherd in the Christmas play *and* I get to do what the shepherds did: tell everyone that Jesus is the best Christmas present ever!"

Christmas joy is sharing love
With everyone you see,
And telling them that Jesus came!
It's how you Otter Be!

Today in the town of David a Savior has been born to you.
He is the Messiah, the Lord.
Luke 2:11

LOOK FOR MORE OTTER B™ BOOKS!

If you loved this book, here are more titles with character-building
lessons and the fun of Otter B™.

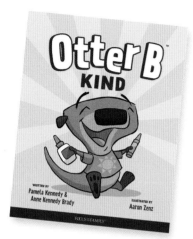
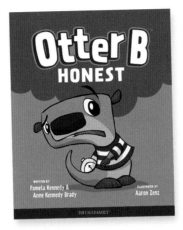

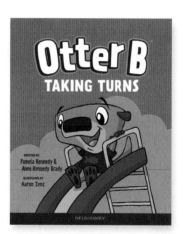

Focus on the Family Clubhouse Jr.® Magazine

Enjoy more faith-filled fun and learning delivered right to your
door. You'll love the way *Clubhouse Jr.* reinforces biblical values
for children ages 3-7. This award-winning kids' magazine promotes
family closeness, and encourages reading and thinking skills. Each
monthly issue is jam-packed with creative Bible stories, exciting
fiction, entertaining nature features, fun puzzles, silly jokes and
more—all designed to give your child a strong spiritual start.
Learning about God should always be this much fun!

FocusOnTheFamily.com/Store